ET. MCKINLEY

MICHAEL'S
NEW HAIRCUT

Written and illustrated by

Karen G. Frandsen

CHILDRENS PRESS ®

CHICAGO

Library of Congress Cataloging-in-Publication Data

Frandsen, Karen G.
    Michael's new haircut.

    Summary: Michael keeps his hat on all day at school
to hide his new, too-short haircut.
[1. Hair—Fiction. 2. Schools—Fiction] I. Title.
PZ7.F8488Mi 1986   [E]   86-11696
ISBN O-516-O3545-2

Michael decided to stay in his closet all day, maybe forever.
His new haircut was too short!

He put signs on his door.

Knock
Keep Out
Do Not Disturb

His mother read the signs. Then she opened the door and said, "It's time for school."

Michael said he was sick.

His mother gave him
his lunch, his jacket, and
a new baseball hat to go
with his new haircut.

She sent him off to school.

When he got to school he decided to keep his new hat on forever. Then no one could tell that his hair was too short.

When his best friend wanted
to try it on, Michael said "NO!"

When his teacher asked him to take it off, he said he had a bad cold and he had to wear it until he was better, which might take a very long time.

When Suzy tried to pull it off, he said she better stop because his hair had bugs and now they were on his hat and they would get on her if she touched it.

At recess Jason wanted him to play ball, but he couldn't because his hat might fall off. Billy wanted him to climb in the cheese castle, but he couldn't because his hat might fall off. So Billy called him a dummy and Jason said he couldn't be his best friend.

When no one was looking,
he pulled Suzy's hair
ribbon. Then he went into
the bathroom alone.

He took off his hat and looked in the mirror.

HIS NEW HAIRCUT WAS STILL TOO SHORT!!

Finally it was time to
go home. Michael lined
up by Suzy.

Suzy tried to kiss him.

YUK!

Then his hat fell off.
Suzy yelled, "Bugs!"

No one even noticed
Michael's new haircut.

The next morning, Michael got ready for school.

He took his lunch, his
jacket, and his new
baseball hat. He knew
his best friend might want
to try it on. Today he
would not wear his hat
all day—his hair was
not too short.

About the author/artist

Karen Frandsen grew up in southern California and presently lives in San Diego with her children, Eric and Ingrid.

Ms. Frandsen is a free-lance artist and elementary school teacher.

The real experiences of her two children and her students are the basis for **Michael's New Haircut.**